The Travels of
ERMINE
(who is very determined)

Stoat
on Stage

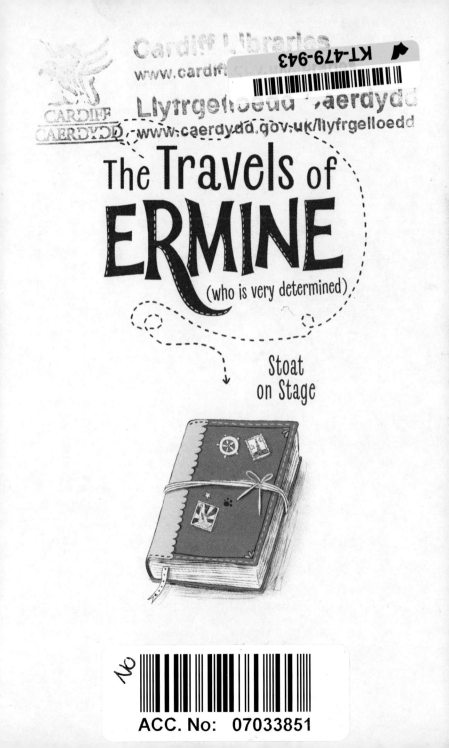

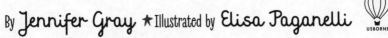
By Jennifer Gray ★ Illustrated by Elisa Paganelli

USBORNE

The Travels of
ERMINE

(who is very determined)

Stoat
on Stage

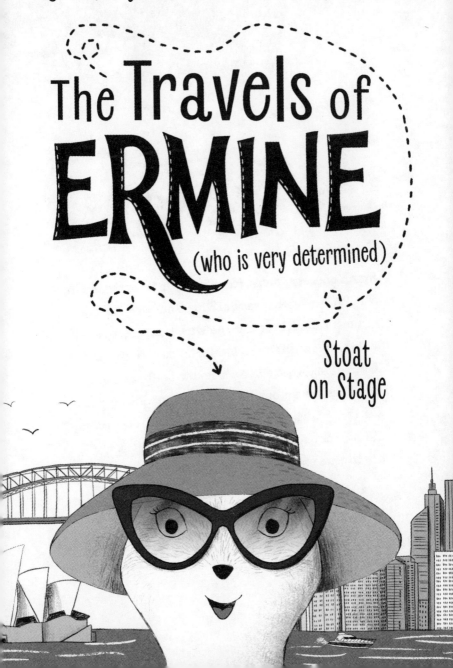

Dear Sylvia,

Thank you very much for offering to have Ermine to stay on her world travels. Since I adopted her she has turned out to be a very determined young lady with a great sense of adventure. I'm sure she and Butterfly will get on like a house on fire! Ermine also likes to help out, so if you need anything fixing she is definitely the one to ask. She will be arriving at half past eleven on Tuesday morning. I've told her to meet you at the Opera House.

With best wishes,

Maria · Grand Duchess Maria Von Schnitzel

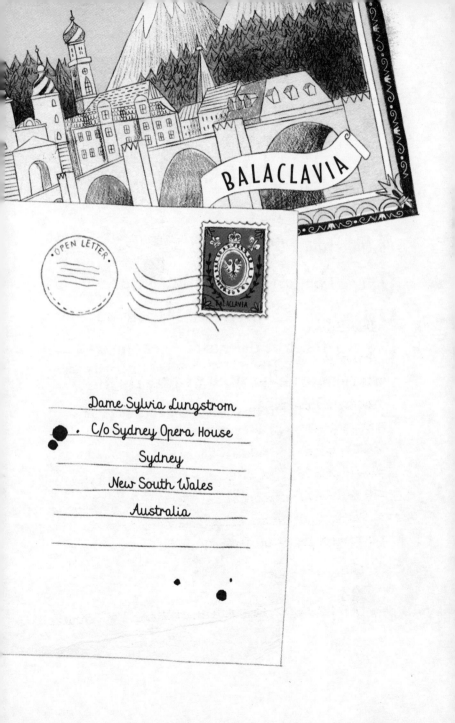

BALACLAVIA

OPEN LETTER

Dame Sylvia Lungstrom
C/o Sydney Opera House
Sydney
New South Wales
Australia

Chapter 1

Sylvia Lungstrom, the world's greatest opera singer, was feeling frazzled. There was only a week left before the curtain went up on her performance at the Sydney Opera House and she was late for rehearsal AGAIN.

The director would be cross. The cast would be cross. And Luciano Singalotti – who was playing the main part opposite her – would probably storm off stage in one of his famous tantrums.

Sylvia was never normally late. But having her eight-year-old granddaughter, Butterfly, to stay for the summer holidays made life much more complicated – especially as Butterfly thought opera sounded like a bunch of hyenas stuck in a dustbin.

Thank goodness she had phoned her old friend, Maria, for advice on what to do, thought Sylvia. And what a stroke of luck that Maria had suggested that Ermine should come and stay as part of her world travels. It would be a wonderful surprise for Butterfly to have a friend to play with, particularly one as unusual as Ermine! Sylvia smiled to herself. She could hardly wait to see the look on her granddaughter's face when their guest arrived.

But meanwhile she had a rehearsal to
go to.

"Please hurry up, Butterfly!" Sylvia
begged. The Opera House stood looking over
the harbour. It was built on a great platform,
like an ancient temple, and Sylvia and
Butterfly had only reached the first level.
There was still another big set of steps to go
before they got to the stage door.

"I don't want to!" Butterfly dragged up
the steps behind her grandmother. She was
a slip of a girl with a gentle face and big, dark
eyes. Right now though, she didn't look
gentle at all. She looked positively ferocious.
Her face wore a big scowl and her thick,
cropped hair poked out in all directions from
under a baseball cap, which she had on back

to front. The baseball cap was denim, like her dungarees and sneakers. She was also wearing odd socks. "I want to climb the bridge."

Sydney Harbour Bridge was probably the city's best-known landmark apart from the Opera House. It formed a great arch over the harbour and Butterfly had set her heart on climbing all the way up to the top of it and all the way down the other side on the famous bridge climb.

"We'll do that later," Sylvia promised.

"But I want to do it now!" Butterfly sat down on the concrete.

"Butterfly…" Sylvia pleaded. "I'm late for rehearsal as it is. I need to practise."

"No, you don't," Butterfly said. "You just need to sing something decent, like Winifred Winnit does." Her face brightened. "Her performing wallabies are **AWESOME!**"

Winifred Winnit was a children's entertainer famous for songs such as "Kevin the Kangaroo" and "Kiss Me, Koala".

To Sylvia's trained ear, it was clear that Winifred Winnit could barely sing a note. But everyone in Australia, including Butterfly, absolutely adored her. Winifred and her wallabies had won the biggest talent show on Australian TV for two years in a row and were hotly tipped to win this year's competition too, which was due to take place in just two days' time:

Australia's
MOST AWESOME
ANIMAL
SHOW

Sylvia had thought it would be fun to get tickets. But since she'd learned about

Ermine's visit, she'd had an even better idea…

Just then she heard a faint pattering behind her.

"Excuse me," said a voice. "I'm looking for Sylvia Lungstrom. Do you know where I can find her? Only this place is enormous and I don't know where to go!"

A brown, furry animal with a long, black-tipped bushy tail, two coal-black eyes, white whiskers and a pink nose stood beside Butterfly. The creature was about as high as Butterfly's knee and was wearing a blue pinafore dress and a straw hat. A camera was slung over its shoulder and in one paw it carried a small bag marked TOOL KIT.

"Ermine!" Sylvia cried with relief. "You're early!"

"Sylvia!" Ermine squeaked. "It's you!" She removed a photograph from her pocket and examined it. "You look just like your picture, except without the horns."

"I only wear those onstage," Sylvia explained. She bent down and regarded Ermine closely. "And you look just like your picture too, except your fur is a different colour."

"It's white in the winter," Ermine told her. "But in the summer it turns brown. We stoats are very clever like that."

"You certainly are!" Sylvia said. "By the way, this is my granddaughter, Butterfly."

Ermine held out a paw. "Hello," she said politely. "I'm Ermine." Then, "Did you fall over or do you just like sitting on the floor?"

Butterfly gawped at her. "You can talk!"

she said. She'd forgotten all about her tantrum.

"Yes, but I can't sing," Ermine said sadly. "At least not as well as your grandmother can." She clasped her paws together and looked up at the Opera House in awe. The roofs of the beautiful building towered above them like a set of billowing sails. "I can't wait to go to the opera and hear you sing, Sylvia," Ermine sighed. "I can wear my feathered hat!"

"Your what?" Butterfly said, getting up.

"My feathered hat," Ermine repeated. "The Duchess gave it to me. She adopted me when I was a kitten. She's taught me all sorts of useful things, like how to fix a bicycle chain and when to wear a feathered hat."

"Where *is* your feathered hat, Ermine?" Sylvia asked.

"With the rest of my luggage," Ermine said. "The taxi driver's bringing it. Look, there she is."

The taxi driver came towards them carrying a stack of small, brightly coloured suitcases.

"You can put them in my dressing room," Sylvia told the taxi driver. She glanced at her watch. "Now I really must get going. Butterfly, you take Ermine to the cafe and get her something to eat…" She paused. "And while you're there, you can work on your act."

"What act?" Butterfly asked.

Sylvia's eyes twinkled. "The one you're going to do for *Australia's Most Awesome Animal Show*. I've entered you both in the talent competition."

"Really?" Butterfly gasped.

"Really." Sylvia smiled. "As long as Ermine agrees."

"Please, Ermine!" Butterfly begged. "I've always wanted to do something like that!"

Ermine didn't have to think about it for long.

A talent show? It sounded exactly the sort of thing she'd be good at. She nodded. "Of course I will. The photographs will look brilliant in my scrapbook! The Duchess said I have to fill it up so I have a record of my travels."

"Yessssssss!" Butterfly high-fived Ermine's paw and gave Sylvia a big hug. Then she bounded down the steps towards the harbour.

"Wait for me!" Ermine chased after her, the sun warming her fur. As she looked out over the blue water she had the feeling this was the start of a **really big ADVENTURE!**

Chapter 2

Beside the pool at Winifred Winnit's luxury house...

Winifred Winnit was lying on a sunbed under an umbrella, sipping a cocktail from a tall glass. Her face was covered in green mud and she had a piece of cucumber over each eye.

On the bed beside her reclined her pet Tasmanian devil – a creature about the size of a small dog, with dark fur, a broad muzzle and very sharp teeth. It had a gold collar around its neck and a pair of reflecting sunglasses perched on its nose.

"This is the life, Cruella!" Winifred said, removing the cucumber from her eyes and addressing her pet Tasmanian devil fondly. "Cheers!"

Cruella crushed the umbrella in her teeth and took a big **slurp** of cocktail.

"Good, isn't it?" Winifred said.

Cruella burped.

Winifred looked around contentedly.
Winnit Mansion was her dream home. It
had everything a TV star could want: a pool,
a tennis court, a cinema room, a popcorn
machine, seven bedrooms – one for each day
of the week – and gold loo seats. It was the
sort of place you never had to leave because
everything was already there.

The only problem was that Winnit Mansion had cost a fortune to build and Winifred had no money left. Which was why she had to win *Australia's Most Awesome Animal Show* one more time. Then she could retire from showbiz and spend the rest of her life doing absolutely nothing.

"The prize money this year is a **MILLION DOLLARS**," she told Cruella. "We can just about manage on that. We could even get a Jacuzzi put in." Her face mask cracked into a sneer. "Better still, we can get rid of those loathsome wallabies *and* we'll never have to see another child again!" She cackled. "Nasty smelly things – and I don't just mean the wallabies."

Cruella growled her agreement.

"I suppose we should rehearse," Winifred groaned. "Although if I have to sing 'Kiss Me, Koala' one more time I think I'll be sick. I mean, who wrote that rubbish?"

Cruella pointed a paw in Winifred's direction.

"Oh yes, you're right – it *was* me," Winifred remembered. "Which obviously means it isn't rubbish, it's brilliant!" She sat up and reached for a towel. The talent show was going to take place in the big concert hall at the Opera House. Over two thousand people would be there, not to mention the fact that it would be beamed live all over the country. It was the perfect opportunity to remind everyone how amazing she was. And she didn't want those stupid wallabies ruining it. "You'd better go and get the wallabies, Cruella," she said. "They need to practise their routine."

Cruella got down off the sun lounger and lumbered off in the direction of a dilapidated shed, which stood some way from the pool in a scruffy enclosure behind a high fence. The shed had several padlocks on the door to stop the wallabies from escaping. Cruella unpicked them one by one with her long toes and pushed the door open.

The wallabies shuffled out. They were similar to kangaroos, only smaller, with strong hind legs, broad feet and a long, thick tail, which made them excellent at hopping. They also had small front legs, which they used for play-boxing in the wild.

Cruella marched
the wallabies out of
the enclosure...

and down
some steps...

into a large basement
area of the house, where
Winifred had built
a rehearsal studio.

Winifred was waiting for them. She had changed into a colourful clown outfit. In place of the green mud, she had painted her face with freckles and warm rosy cheeks. Her blue eyes were framed with long fake lashes and on her head was a bright pink wig.

"All right, wallabies," she snapped. "Get into position or no dinner."

The wallabies formed a neat line behind her and linked tails.

Winifred pressed the remote.

The joyful sound of happy music filled
the room as the wallabies began to sway to
and fro. Winifred forced her face into a smile
and began to sing in a baby voice:

"My mummy bought me a cuddly bear,
It sleeps upon my bed,
It's got grey fur and a fluffy tail,
And a square-shaped
sort of head.
Its nose is black and
its eyes are round,
And it lives in a
big gum tree,
Oh I love my koala
and I know my koala
loves me!"

Winifred's smile evaporated. She pressed PAUSE.

"MORE ENERGY!" she screamed at the wallabies. "DO SOME ACROBATICS!"

The wallabies bounced about. Two of them fetched unicycles. The others began to form a wallaby pyramid.

Winifred pressed PLAY.

"So kiss me, koala, you know I love you so...
From your square-shaped head to your fluffy tail,
I don't want you to go.
Stay on my bed while I'm asleep,
We make a brilliant team..."

The smallest wallaby took a run-up.

"If you kiss me, koala, I'll have a lovely dream!"

The wallaby landed perfectly on top of the pyramid on the tip of its tail.

Winifred gave the pretend audience a wink, rested her cheek on her hands in a gesture of sleep and closed her eyes.

The music stopped.

Winifred's eyes flew open again. "Not bad," she told the wallabies. "Now get lost."

The wallabies shuffled out with Cruella.

Winifred watched them go. She smiled to herself. She, Winifred, was as fabulous as ever, and there wasn't another animal in the whole of Australia who could beat her performing wallabies. The kids would go wild. There was no doubt about it: the prize money was in the bag.

Chapter 3

At the quayside in Sydney Harbour...

"I'm starving," Butterfly said to Ermine as they made their way to the cafe by the water. "Let's have brunch."

"What's brunch?" asked Ermine.

"It's a cross between breakfast and lunch," Butterfly explained. "Everyone has it in Australia."

Ermine thought for a minute. "Do they have lea as well?"

"What's lea?"

"A cross between lunch and tea."

Butterfly giggled. "No, silly, just brunch."
She led the way to a table at the waterside.

Ermine leaped onto the chair beside her
and admired the view.

Ferries ran to and fro, sailing boats bobbed
on the sparkling blue water and crowds of
people walked along the wide promenade.

Behind them, the city's skyscrapers rose up
into the clear, blue sky. Ermine thought she
had never seen anything so spectacular. It was
a world away from the snow-topped mountains
of Balaclavia. It was also much hotter. Ermine
was glad of her straw hat.

The waiter came over. "What can I get you, Butterfly?"

"Corn fritters with syrup and bacon on the side for two, please," said Butterfly.

The waiter went to place their order.

"What exactly is a corn fritter?" asked Ermine curiously. The Duchess had told her it was good to try different types of food when you travelled.

"It's a sort of cake made out of sweetcorn," Butterfly told her. "Trust me – you'll love it!"

A cake made out of sweetcorn? *Now that was unusual,* thought Ermine. When she and the Duchess made cakes at the castle it was always a Victoria sponge.

Very soon the food arrived. Ermine tucked

in. Butterfly was right: the corn fritters tasted delicious and the bacon and syrup gave them a sticky salty-sweet flavour.

"What do you eat in Balaclavia?" Butterfly asked her.

"I normally have eggs for breakfast," said Ermine, licking syrup off her whiskers,

"and rabbit stew for tea. I like fish too, especially if I catch it fresh from the river. What about you?"

"I eat *tons* of fish," said Butterfly, "and rice and noodles. My dad's Vietnamese. He does most of the cooking when I'm at home." She beamed proudly. "And I get to help."

"How come you're *not* at home?" asked Ermine. "Are you on your world travels, like me?"

Butterfly giggled. "No, silly! It's the holidays. Grandma offered to have me to stay. Anyway, how come *you* live with a duchess?"

"The Duke trapped me!" Ermine told her. "He wanted to use my fur to trim the collar of his robe!"

"But why?" Butterfly was shocked.

Ermine sighed. "It's very precious, my fur. It's called ermine, like me." She leaned forward to tell the story. "You see in the old days, when Balaclavia still had a king, the Duke and

Duchess had to wear it round their necks when they went to visit His Majesty at the palace."

"That's horrible!" Butterfly said indignantly.

Ermine nodded sadly. "I know. The Duchess never liked it – she always said the only place for ermine is on a stoat. She didn't mind when the people got rid of the king. But the Duke was still very attached to his fur collar, which is why he caught me. Luckily the Duchess got back to the castle just in time to rescue me or I wouldn't be sitting here now."

"The Duchess sounds really nice," Butterfly said. "You should buy her a present from Australia to say thank you."

"That's a good idea!" said Ermine. "She needs a new hat. She spent all her savings on buying my round-the-world air ticket!" Her face fell. "But I don't have any money."

"You will have when we win the talent show!" Butterfly said. "Stay here. I'll go and get a pen and paper so we can write down some ideas for our act."

Butterfly disappeared inside the cafe.

As soon as she had gone, Ermine heard an incredible sound coming from somewhere nearby.

NYOW-WOW-WA-NYOW-WOW-WA-NYOW-WOW-WA

The sound reverberated up her tail and right through her body all the way to the tips of her whiskers. She found herself tapping her feet in time to the beat. Before she knew it, she had climbed down off her chair and run over to where the music was coming from on the quay.

She cast off her straw hat and started to dance.

NYOW-WOW-WA NYOW-WOW-WA NYOW-WOW-WA

Ermine flipped...

...and somersaulted.

She cartwheeled...

...and jumped.

She even did the **worm**.

The music stopped.

She heard clapping. To

her surprise, a crowd had

gathered to watch her.

"That was pretty good," she heard a man say to her, as the rest of the people wandered away. "I've never seen a weasel dance to the didgeridoo before."

"I'm NOT a weasel, I'm a stoat," Ermine bristled. "And we're very good at dancing – it's what we do in the wild." She looked up. The man had dark skin, black, curly hair that fell around his shoulders and a broad, kind face. In fact, he looked so kind that she decided to forgive him.

"True ay: you are very good!" He smiled.
"I'm Eric."

"And I'm Ermine," said Ermine.

"And by the way, what *is* a didgeridoo?"

"This is." Eric patted a long
wooden tube, which was
propped up against his chair.
The tube was about a
metre and a half long, made
from a textured wood and
earthy in colour.
Ermine examined
it carefully.

"The didgeridoo is one of the world's oldest musical instruments," Eric told her. "It's Aboriginal, like me. It makes the sound of nature – you know, the trees and the animals and the earth."

"It *does* remind me a bit of the forest in Balaclavia where I come from," Ermine said thoughtfully, "when the wind howls or the trees creak, or the animals call…"

Just then she heard Butterfly calling her name.

"That's Butterfly," Ermine said to Eric. "I'd better go. It was really great to meet you."

"It was great to meet you too," said Eric.

The two of them said goodbye.

Ermine went back to the table.

"There you are!" said Butterfly. "I wondered where you'd gone." She picked up the pen and paper. "Now, tell me what you're good at."

Ermine gave Butterfly a few examples. Butterfly wrote them down carefully.

- ☐ Climbing
- ☐ Fishing
- ☐ Swimming
- ☐ Tobogganing
- ☐ Mending bicycles
- ☐ Solving diamond robberies

Butterfly looked at the list. "They're not acts!" she complained. "I meant singing or acrobatics, or something people normally do on talent shows!"

Ermine's eyes flashed. "Well," she said, a little stiffly, "climbing *is* acrobatic. At least, it is when *I* do it."

"I suppose…" said Butterfly.

"Maybe you're just not very good at it," Ermine suggested.

"Of course I am!" Butterfly responded. "I LOVE climbing."

"Trees?" asked Ermine, thinking of the pine forests in Balaclavia.

"No, bridges," Butterfly said.

"*Bridges?*" Ermine echoed, her curiosity aroused. She'd never heard of anyone climbing bridges before. "What bridges?"

"That one." Butterfly pointed to the

Sydney Harbour Bridge. "Grandma
promised to take me this afternoon. You can
come too! It'll be good practice if we do an
acrobatic show. We need to get used to heights."

Ermine looked up at the enormous bridge.
She could see a group of people making their
way slowly along one of the metal arches
towards the summit. They were so high up
that they looked like ants.

She considered for a moment. "Can I get a photo at the top for my scrapbook?" she asked.

"Of course you can!" said Butterfly.

Ermine's whiskers twitched. She was never one to say no to a challenge. "All right," she agreed. "I'll do it."

Chapter 4

That afternoon on Sydney Harbour Bridge...

Ermine was perched on a narrow metal walkway high above the harbour. She was dressed in a blue boiler suit, with a headband to hold her ears back. The boiler suit had come from a doll in the souvenir shop, as there wasn't a suit small enough for her to borrow.

Luckily it fitted perfectly!

Butterfly was at the front of the line, followed by Sylvia and Ermine. The rest of the group followed behind them, all wearing the same blue boiler suits with a rope clipped on

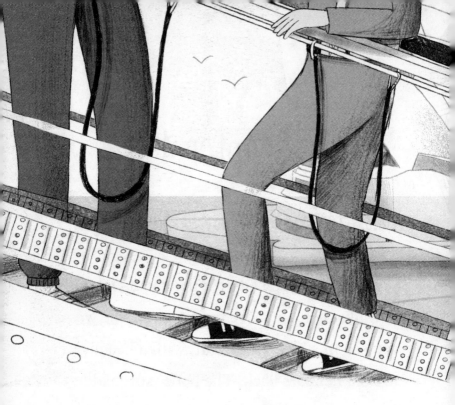

at the waist. The other end of each rope was
attached to a safety rail so they couldn't fall off.

Ermine wished the Duchess could see her
now. She felt very grown up and very brave!
She peeped down. The sea was a distant blue.
They were already so high up that it was the

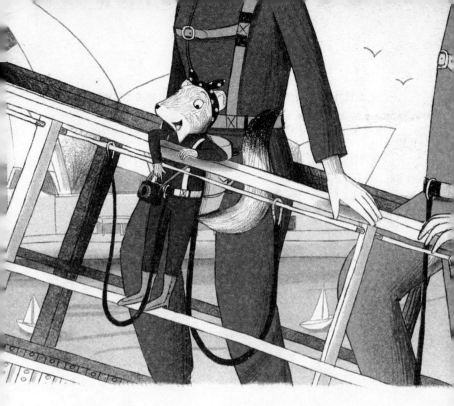

people on the quay below who looked like
ants now. And they had barely even started
the climb!

"Are you ready?" the guide asked.

"READY!" everyone shouted.

"Then let's go," said the guide.

Ermine leaped up the steps after Sylvia.
It was tough going for someone so small.
The higher they got, the windier it became.

"HELP!" she squeaked as the wind
battered her whiskers.

But nobody heard her –
the wind was too strong.

"HELP!" she cried again.

No one paid any attention.

wHOOSH! Suddenly a great gust knocked her sideways. It blew her under the safety rail and off the bridge. Sylvia screamed at the top of her mighty opera-singer's voice. The sound was deafening. Even the wind seemed to stop for a few seconds.

Ermine dangled helplessly beneath the metal steps on the end of the rope.

"HOLD ON, ERMINE!" cried Butterfly.

"I'LL HELP." She crouched down and reached under the safety rail to grab the rope, ready to pull Ermine up.

"WAIT!" shouted the guide.

But it was too late.

WHOOOOSH!

There was an even stronger gust of wind.

Sylvia screamed again, even louder.

This time it was Butterfly who got knocked under the safety rail and off the bridge! She dangled beside Ermine.

The guide leaned over the rail while the rest of the group huddled together in fright.

"DON'T WORRY," she shouted. "WE'LL HAVE YOU SAFE AND SOUND IN NO TIME. JUST HANG ON WHILE I CALL FOR BACK-UP."

She got out her walkie-talkie.

But Butterfly wasn't worried.

"Hey, Ermine," she said, "we could do a trapeze act in the talent show. Check this out!" She began swinging backwards and forwards on the rope with all her might.

"*Wheeeeee!*" she cried, zipping to and fro.

"Wheeeeeeeeeeeeeeeeee! Wheeeeeeeeeeeeeeeee eeeeeeeeeeeee!"

Just then there was a ripping sound.

Ermine gasped. Where the rope clipped onto Butterfly's boiler suit, the cloth had begun to tear. "Butterfly!" she squeaked.

"Your suit's ripping. Stay still!" Butterfly froze. But she couldn't stop the rope from swinging, or the boiler suit from tearing.

RRRRIP!

The tear in the cloth was getting bigger.

Sylvia's anxious face appeared above them, surrounded by the other members of the group. "DO SOMETHING, ERMINE!" she pleaded. "BUTTERFLY MIGHT FALL!"

Ermine glanced at the dizzying drop beneath them. She had to act fast. Suddenly she remembered her tool kit. Her face took on a determined expression. She knew exactly what to do. "DON'T WORRY, SYLVIA," she called back. "I'LL SAVE HER!"

The next time Butterfly swung by,
Ermine reached out with her front paws
and made a grab for the girl's foot...

SNATCH!

The two of them swung
backwards and forwards together on the
end of their ropes. It really *was* like a trapeze
act, thought Ermine, who had once been to
the circus with the Duchess. Only there
was no safety net. She had to hurry.

She wriggled her way up Butterfly's leg…

SQUIRM!

And into her pocket…

PLOP!

From there she pulled the tool kit out of her own boiler suit, opened it carefully and felt inside.

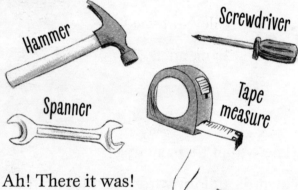

Hammer

Screwdriver

Spanner

Tape measure

Ah! There it was!

Needle and thread.

Quick as a flash, Ermine threaded the needle. She bit the cotton with her sharp teeth and tied a knot in the end. Then she began to sew.

Stitch! Stitch! Stitch! Stitch! Stitch!

Up and down flew her paw…

Up and down and in and out…

In tiny, neat stitches…

Until the tear in

Butterfly's boiler suit was

well and truly mended.

"Hooray!" sang Sylvia. "Ermine's done it! She's saved Butterfly! She really *is* Australia's most awesome animal!"

"HOORAY!" shouted the group. Everyone up on the bridge hugged one another in delight.

"Where did you learn to do that?" Butterfly asked Ermine in amazement.

"The Duchess taught me, of course!" said Ermine, ducking back down into Butterfly's pocket to get out of the wind. It was bending her whiskers!

Just then they felt a pull on the rope. A team of guides had arrived. Very soon they were hauled to safety on the bridge. The group of climbers clapped and cheered.

"Oh, Butterfly! Thank goodness you're

safe!" Sylvia enveloped her granddaughter
in her arms. For once, Butterfly didn't
complain. She hugged Sylvia as hard as
she could.

"Mind me!" said a small voice.

Sylvia stepped back.

Ermine poked her head out of
Butterfly's pocket,
looking a little
squashed.

"Maybe we won't do acrobatics in the show after all," Butterfly said.

"I think that's a very good idea," agreed Sylvia.

"So do I," said Ermine. "I really don't think Butterfly's good enough at climbing yet." She straightened her whiskers. "Could someone please take a photograph?" she asked the group. "Only I'd like to put it in my scrapbook to show the Duchess."

Chapter 5

Later that evening at Winnit Mansion...

Winifred Winnit was standing in front of a mirror practising her acceptance speech for winning *Australia's Most Awesome Animal Show*, when her computer began to ping.

PING
PING
PING
PING
PING

Winifred frowned. That meant people were talking about the competition on social media.

And they weren't just talking about it – they were going nuts!

Curses! she thought. One of her rivals must have posted something. She wondered which one it could be.

Paul Piggott and
Pete the percussion-
playing platypus?

Lucy Sponge
and Sue the
sighing sloth?

Bill Trogg and
Bert the bearded
tarantula?

Probably Bill Trogg, Winifred decided. Posting some pathetic piffle about his awful arachnid was just the sort of dirty, low-life trick that big-headed boaster would use to get publicity. She snorted. As if Bill Trogg and his tarantula could beat Winifred Winnit and her performing wallabies to a million dollar prize! The idea was ridiculous. All that spider did was crawl about.

PING PING PING PING

AUSTRALIA NEWS

DARING STOAT IS NEW DARLING OF SYDNEY!
Is Ermine Australia's Most Awesome Animal?

Winifred reached for the computer and scrolled through the posts. Her face went pale.

It wasn't Bill Trogg and his bearded tarantula everyone was going crazy about.

The internet was abuzz with stories about some revolting child called Butterfly and – Winifred could hardly believe it – Ermine, a sewing *stoat*.

AUSTRALIA NEWS

DARING STOAT IS NEW DARLING OF SYDNEY!
Is Ermine Australia's Most Awesome Animal?

Winifred almost fainted.

AUSTRALIA NEWS Financ

Sydney today witnessed one of the most extraordinary events in its entire history when Ermine, a brave young stoat, came to the rescue of Butterfly Lungstrom, the granddaughter of our very own opera star, Dame Sylvia.

The three of them were taking part in Sydney's famous bridge climb experience when Ermine and then Butterfly were blown off the bridge by high winds.

She forced herself to read on.

When the stitching around Butterfly's safety clip began to tear, Ermine saved her life in a dazzling display of speed darning.

Butterfly (8) has confirmed that they will be entering Australia's Most Awesome Animal Show but they haven't yet decided on their act.

Ermine was not available for comment but, judging by the incredible response to Ermine's exploits, she and Butterfly must already be hot favourites to win. Last year's winners – Winifred Winnit and her performing wallabies – had better watch out!

Winifred Winnit ground her teeth. *Not available for comment!* What a stupid thing to say! Of course the stoat wasn't available for comment – that was because it couldn't speak! A stoat was just another dumb animal, like all the rest of them, even if it *could* sew.

She clicked angrily on a video link. One of the other climbers in the group had filmed the whole episode.

Butterfly and Ermine dangled from the bridge. *"DO SOMETHING, ERMINE!"* came a voice – Sylvia Lungstrom's, thought Winifred, judging by the volume. She saw the stoat's face take on a determined expression.

"DON'T WORRY, SYLVIA, I'LL SAVE HER!" it said.

IT COULD TALK??!!!!!!!!! Winifred's jaw dropped. Her eyes popped. She sat through the

rest of the
video in a daze.

Just then
Cruella pottered
in, looking for
food. When she
saw Ermine on the
computer screen, she
growled. Then she picked
up a cushion in her gigantic teeth and shook
it until all the feathers came out.

Winifred snapped out of her trance. She
jumped to her feet and kicked the feathers in the
air. "Stupid, sewing stoat! Thinks it can steal
my prize, does it? We'll see about that! I'll…I'll…"

Winifred paused for a moment.

What would she do?

Then she had an idea. A sewing stoat would come in very handy about the house, especially one that had a tail like a duster. She would find it, catch it and make it work for its keep.

"Quick, Cruella!" she snapped. "Get the dressing-up box. We'll need a disguise if we're going to catch it."

Winifred had a very large collection of dressing-up clothes, mainly thanks to all the children's parties she had entertained at before she became famous. Cruella dragged over a large trunk they were kept in and threw open the lid with her snout. Then she leaped into it and started to hurl its contents all over the room.

Winifred picked up a few things to examine them before tossing them aside impatiently.

Dorothy
and Toto

Goldilocks
and the one bear

Kangaroo
and joey

Little Red Riding Hood
and the wolf

Little Bo Peep and a sheep

"No! No! No!"

Winifred cried. "That
Butterfly girl looks far too
smart to fall for any of those.
She mustn't suspect anything. We
need to blend in with the crowd."

Cruella burrowed deeper.
Costumes littered the room.

"Wait!" Winifred said.
She picked one up off the floor.

Surfer dude and dog...

"This is perfect, Cruella!" Winifred cried. She tried on the wig and glasses and admired herself in the mirror. She looked so dude-like, even her keenest fan wouldn't recognize her. She gave an evil chuckle. All they had to do now was follow Butterfly and Ermine, wait until the child's back was turned, then

nab the stoat and keep it hard at work until the talent show was over and they were winners – by which time Winnit

Mansion would be lovely and clean as well.

Winifred was so happy she felt a new song coming on.

Easy, peasy. Ermine squeezy!
Catch the stoat and make it squeegee,
Use its tail to dust down low,
While Winifred wins the talent show!

There was just one thing she needed to do. Winifred picked up the phone and dialled the number of her agent.

"Gustav? Is that you? Now listen carefully. I need some information. I want you to find out where Sylvia Lungstrom lives…"

Chapter 6

The next morning at Sylvia's house...

Ermine and Butterfly were having breakfast in the garden. The house was a twenty-minute ferry ride from Sydney Harbour, perched on a hill overlooking the ocean. Beneath them lay a pretty, sheltered cove full of crystal-clear water where a few sailing boats were moored. Ermine would have liked to go and explore. But that would have to wait: the show was tomorrow and they still didn't have an act.

Butterfly was looking through Ermine's list of talents. She had already crossed out *climbing*.

The next one of Ermine's talents was fishing.

- ☒ Climbing
- ☐ Fishing
- ☐ Swimming
- ☐ Tobogganing
- ☐ Mending bicycles
- ☐ Solving diamond robberies

"That's not a bad idea," Butterfly mused. "We could get a giant tank of fish and see how many you can catch. I could cook them," she added excitedly. "I *love* cooking! That could be my talent! We can work together."

"All right," said Ermine, popping a delicious piece of mango into her mouth and chewing it with relish. "But I might need a bit of practice. I haven't been fishing since I started my world travels."

Butterfly beamed. "I know just the place," she said. "I'll ask Grandma if she can drop us off on her way to rehearsal."

A little while later Ermine sat on the top deck of a ferry with Sylvia and Butterfly, shielded by her straw hat. She was taking snaps with her camera to paste into her scrapbook. The ferry took them past all sorts of interesting places. She hoped she'd be able to visit them after the talent show.

Botanic
Gardens

National Maritime Museum

Luna Park

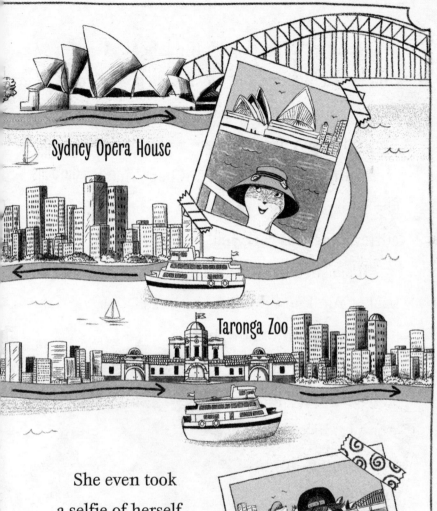

Sydney Opera House

Taronga Zoo

She even took
a selfie of herself
and Butterfly!

"Here we are!"
said Butterfly.

The three of them got off the boat. A surfer dude with big hair and a bandana got off too. He was with a small, black, muscly dog with a long tail. Both of them were wearing shades.

Ermine stared at them. "What's that for?" she whispered. She pointed at the board the surfer dude was carrying.

"It's a surfboard, silly," Butterfly whispered back. "You know, for riding waves."

Ermine didn't know, but it sounded fun anyway – she imagined it was a bit like tobogganing, but on water instead of snow.

"I'll show you how to do it later when we go to the beach," Butterfly promised. They got into the ticket queue for the aquarium. So did the surfer dude and his dog. Sylvia bought them tickets. "I'll send Derek, my housekeeper, to collect you," she promised. "Then this evening I want to hear all about your act and see the dress rehearsal. You need to be prepared for tomorrow!" She waved goodbye and got back on the ferry to the Opera House. The sound of Sylvia practising her scales washed around the bay.

Ermine and Butterfly went into the
aquarium, followed by the surfer
dude and his dog.

Ermine gazed at the huge
fish tanks with astonishment.
She had never seen so many
species of fish, or realized that
they could come in so many
shapes and sizes and colours.

"What are those?" she asked,
pointing to a tank full of pale,
floating balloon-like
creatures.

"They look easy to catch."

"Don't be daft," said Butterfly.
"They're jellyfish – they'll sting you."

"What about these?" The next tank
contained flat triangular fish with long tails.

"Definitely not," said Butterfly. "They're
stingrays. They'll sting you even worse."

They went into a tunnel. Ermine's eyes
widened. It was like being underneath the sea!
Above her, shoals of silver fish swished
this way and that.

"I could catch those," she suggested,
pointing at the silver fish.

Butterfly snorted. "Sure! If you
want to get eaten by a shark!"

A huge, snarling grey fish with beady,
black eyes and a jagged fin swam towards them.

Ermine jumped back. "No, thank you!"
she said.

The tunnel ended. Butterfly dashed
forwards towards the next section. "Come on,
Ermine!" she said. "It's the rock pool!"

"Rock pool?" Ermine queried, scurrying
after her.

"You know," said Butterfly, "it's the fun
bit where we're allowed to touch the fish."
She dashed up to the attendant. "Excuse me,"
she said politely, "would it be all right if
Ermine practised her fishing? It's for
Australia's Most Awesome Animal Show –
we're trying to work out our act."

The attendant grinned. He recognized
Butterfly and Ermine from the rescue on
the bridge. "No worries," he said to Ermine.

"As long as you promise to be careful and put everything back and not hurt it."

"I promise!" Ermine said solemnly.

Ermine climbed up to the edge of the rock pool and looked down. As well as lots of little fish, there were all sorts of other interesting things she'd only ever seen in the Duchess's encyclopaedia before.

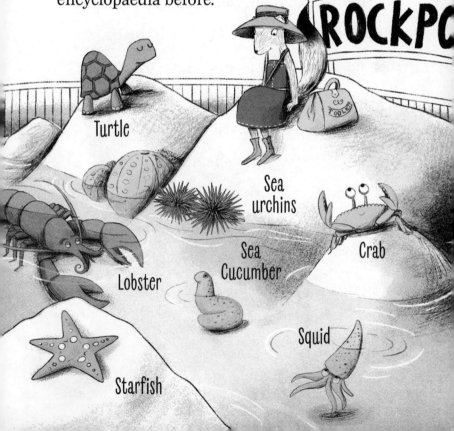

Turtle

Sea
urchins

Crab

Sea
Cucumber

Lobster

Squid

Starfish

Ermine leaned over. She fished about in the rock pool with her paw and gently pulled out a squid.

"Good catch!" said Butterfly.

Ermine wasn't so sure. The squid didn't look very pleased to be disturbed.

"LOOK OUT!" shouted the attendant.

A great cloud of ink squirted from the squid.

Ermine ducked just in time. She didn't want her fur to get dirty!

"YEEEEOOOOWWWWW!"

Ermine looked up. It was the surfer dude! He had propped his surfboard against the wall and was standing right next to her with his dog. He had taken off his sunglasses, and his eyes were now dripping with black squid ink! *What a silly place to stand,* thought Ermine.

She carefully returned the angry squid to the water.

"Try a crab," suggested the attendant.

"Okay."

Ermine pounced on a crab. Only she was so shocked when she held it up and saw its two eyes staring back at her on stalks, she accidentally dropped it.

The crab landed on the surfer dude's dog. It nipped its nose as hard as it could.

"RRRAAOOOWW!"

squealed the dog.

The dog too! thought Ermine. *You'd think
it would move when it saw what happened to
its owner.*

She picked the crab up carefully and put
it back in the pool.

"Have another go," said
the attendant.

This time Ermine went
for the sea cucumber.
Only it was so slippery
that it shot straight out of
her paws and

landed
on the surfer
dude's forehead.

SPLAT!

The surfer dude stood rooted to the spot. The sea cucumber slid slowly down his cheek before dropping back in the pool and drifting calmly away to safety.

Some people just don't learn! Ermine thought.

The surfer dude's face was streaked black from the squid ink and was covered in slime. He looked as if he was dressed up for a Halloween party. Ermine felt the urge to giggle.

The attendant stepped forward with a packet of wet wipes. "No worries, mate. We'll have that off in a jiffy," he said. He began dabbing at the surfer dude's face.

To Ermine's surprise, the surfer dude pushed the attendant roughly away.

"*Get off me!*" he hissed, taking a giant
step backwards – which was when he
tripped over the dog and fell over the barrier
into the rock pool.

"OOOWOWWWWWWWW!"

he howled.

"Oh dear," Butterfly said, "I think he sat on a sea urchin."

"I hope it's all right," Ermine said in a worried voice, peering into the rock pool.

"It will be," the attendant reassured her.

The surfer dude plucked the sea urchin from his tattered wetsuit and placed it back in the pool. He climbed awkwardly over the barrier, collected his surfboard and limped painfully past Ermine and Butterfly towards the exit, leaving a trail of drips in his wake.

Underneath the wet suit the surfer dude

was wearing a pair of bright pink, frilly knickers.

Ermine thought they looked most unsuitable for surfing.

"Do you want to help me feed the sharks?" the attendant asked hopefully. Butterfly shook her head. "We'd better go," she said.

"Thanks for letting me practise," said Ermine.

"No worries," said the attendant. "Good luck with the competition! I hope you win!"

Ermine and Butterfly made their way to the exit to meet Derek.

"Maybe fishing's not such a good idea after all," Ermine sighed.

"I agree," said Butterfly. "But what are we going to do instead?"

"Let's go to the beach," Ermine suggested. Her black eyes sparkled with excitement. "We can have another think about it there, while you're teaching me to surf."

Chapter 7

That afternoon at the beach...

Winifred Winnit sat on the beach, keeping
watch through a pair of binoculars. She
was still wearing the remains of the surfer
dude outfit. Her wetsuit was full of holes
where the sea urchin had
spiked it, her eyes stung
from the squid ink and
her skin felt slimy.

Cruella lay beside
Winifred, nursing her
sore nose.

Butterfly was teaching Ermine how to surf. The two of them were getting used to their boards in the shallows, away from the strong waves further out to sea.

The problem for Winifred was that there were lots of other people around. The spot Ermine and Butterfly had chosen was right in front of the lifeguards' enclosure, where it was safe to swim. And there was a grown-up nearby, keeping an eye on them.

"*Curses!*" Winifred zoomed in with the binoculars. "We have to catch that senseless stoat!" The cheek of the animal was breathtaking. How dare it do all those awful things to her at the aquarium and not even apologize? And then for the stoat just to head to the beach and start swimming without a care in the world. Winifred gnashed her teeth. She was more determined to win the talent show than ever. She had to have that Jacuzzi. She just had to!

Suddenly, an announcement came over the tannoy.

"WOULD ALL THE COMPETITORS IN TODAY'S JUNIOR SUPER SURFER COMPETITION PLEASE MAKE THEIR WAY TO THE LIFEGUARD ENCLOSURE IMMEDIATELY."

Ermine and Butterfly got out of the water with the other kids and lined up in front of the lifeguard tent.

Easy, peasy, Ermine squeezy...

Winifred's eyes gleamed. An idea began to form in her mind. If Ermine was entering the contest, she would be out there on the water surfing all alone. This was their opportunity to grab her. *But how?* She, Winifred, couldn't very well enter a kids' surfing competition. It would attract too much attention. And even though she looked the part (apart from the frilly knickers), she wasn't a very strong swimmer...

Just then, Winifred spied another tent further down the beach.

Pedalos → for Hire

"Come on, Cruella." Winifred sprinted along the beach to the pedalo tent. It was closed. There was a line of blue pedalos chained up outside. "Quick, Cruella!" she hissed.

Cruella opened her jaws wide and bit straight through the chain with her enormous teeth.

"Good work!" Winifred pulled one of the pedalos free. Then she hauled it along the sand to the water's edge and jumped in.

Cruella jumped in after her.

The two of them pedalled furiously through the surf.

SPLASH! SPLASH! SPLASH! SPLASH!

Out on the water, the Junior Super Surfer Competition was in full swing. The kids had paddled out to sea on their surfboards and were shooting this way and that on the breaking waves. But to Winifred's confusion, Ermine and Butterfly were not among them. Now what were they doing?

Winifred raked the sea with her binoculars. "There they are!" she said.

Ermine and Butterfly had paddled further out. They seemed to be waiting for something.

"Step on the gas, Cruella!" Winifred steered the pedalo towards them, her thighs burning from the exercise. All of a sudden, the pain in her legs eased. The tide was sucking the pedalo out to sea, away from the beach. Very soon, Winifred and Cruella drew level with their targets.

Ha ha! thought Winifred. This was going to be easier than she'd imagined. Butterfly and Ermine hadn't even noticed their approach. Butterfly was too busy pointing at something on the horizon.

To Winifred's surprise, Cruella began to whimper. "What's wrong with you?" she snapped.

Cruella pointed a paw in the same direction as Butterfly. Winifred turned round to have a look. She blinked.

An enormous wave was forming.

Winifred felt the pedalo being
lifted up. The sea became a hill,
then a mountain. The water fell
away beneath them in a vertical
slope. The pedalo teetered on the
crest of the huge wave.

Winifred's mouth formed a
very large O.

Cruella gave a terrified yelp.

"WOOHOOO!"

"WOOHOO!"

Just then Butterfly whizzed past
them on her surfboard. So did Ermine.
The two of them hurtled down the
mountain of water like skiers in a race
– Butterfly ahead by a whisker.

"WHOOOOAAAAA

The pedalo plunged after them, lurching from side to side. Winifred and Cruella clung on for dear life.

Above them the wall of water began to curve. Very soon, the wave curled into a tunnel.

Butterfly and Ermine zipped along it, neck and neck.

The pedalo careered after them.

Winifred and Cruella bounced off the edges of the tunnel of water.

They neared the shore.

wHOOOSH!

Butterfly and Ermine shot
through the end of the wave
and glided elegantly onto the
beach to wild applause from
the other competitors.

CRASH!

The wave finally broke.
A massive dump of churning white
surf swallowed the pedalo, rolling it
over and over and over on the sand.
Winifred and Cruella staggered
from the sea and collapsed.

They looked terrible. Winifred's wetsuit ballooned with water. Her wig was back to front (not to mention her knickers). Cruella's short fur was plastered with evil-smelling seaweed. A small crab was attached to one ear.

Winifred spat the sand out of her mouth. "That's IT," she fumed. "It's time to play dirty."

Chapter 8

The next morning, back at Sylvia's house...

Sydney
AUSTRALIA

Er-mazing
Ermine!

Super stoat set for stardom!

Ermine sat at the table, pasting photos into her scrapbook. The newspapers were full of her success at the Junior Super Surfer Competition the day before.

Ermine sighed. All the newspapers said she and Butterfly were bound to win *Australia's Most Awesome Animal Show*. There was just one small problem: the competition was that afternoon at two thirty and she and Butterfly still hadn't decided on their act. None of their talents seemed quite right for the show. Acrobatics was out. So was fishing and cooking. And even though they were both *spectacularly* good at surfing, they couldn't very well do that onstage, or tobogganing for that matter as there wasn't any snow.

Just then Butterfly came into the kitchen. She was wearing pyjamas, a baseball cap, odd slippers and a big frown from having been woken up early by Sylvia. She plonked herself down at the table and reached for the cereal. Then she removed Ermine's list of talents from under her cap.

Climbing ☒
Fishing ☒
Swimming ☒
Tobogganing ☒
Mending bicycles ☐
Solving diamond robberies ☐

"What about mending bicycles?" Ermine said. "I'm pretty good at that."

"Boring!" said Butterfly. "And there aren't any diamond robberies to solve." She crossed those out as well. "What else could we do?"

Ermine thought about all the things the Duchess had taught her. "We could show people how to put up shelves," she suggested, "or polish a table with beeswax or make a feathered hat."

"Even more boring!" said Butterfly.

Ermine frowned. Butterfly was in a bad mood. The Duchess called it "getting out of bed on the wrong side".

"What about breakdancing?" said Butterfly.

"That's a good idea," Ermine said. "Stoats are brilliant at dancing."

"Says who?" said Butterfly curiously.

"Lots of people," Ermine replied.

"Like who?" Butterfly insisted.

"Like…" Ermine tried to think.

Wait a minute! Her black eyes gleamed with excitement. *Of course!* She knew exactly what they could do for the show – Butterfly had given her a **fantastic** idea.

"**LIKE ERIC!**" she squeaked. "That's IT, Butterfly! We can ask Eric to play for us at the show while we dance." She did a cartwheel across the kitchen table.

"Who's Eric?" asked Butterfly.

"The man I met on the quay when you went to get the notepad at the cafe," Ermine explained. "He plays the didgeridoo. It's the sound of nature. That's why I liked it so much – it reminded me of the forest in Balaclavia. So I started dancing and Eric said I was pretty good for a weasel and I told him I was a stoat and everyone clapped."

"Why on earth didn't you say so before, silly?" cried Butterfly. "That sounds amazing. I'll get Grandma." She rushed off upstairs.

Just then Ermine heard something drop through the letter box in the hall. She went to pick it up. To her surprise, the envelope was addressed to her. She slit it open with her claw and pulled out a piece of thick white paper.

Ermine blinked. It was from Winifred Winnit.

Dear Ermine,

Welcome to Sydney!
I am ~~dead livid~~ delighted that you are taking ~~over~~ part in Australia's Most Awesome Animal Show this year. Seeing as how you were brought up by a duchess and can talk (~~curse~~ clever you!), me and my pet Tasmanian devil, Cruella, would like to ~~eat~~ meet you before the show. Come to the ~~cage~~ stage door at 2 p.m. The wallabies are quite ~~tiresome~~ timid, so please come alone. Don't tell ~~Caterpillar~~ Butterfly.
      Catch you soon!
      Winifred Winnit

PS Sorry I am not very good at ~~singing~~ spelling.

Ermine wondered what she should do. On the one paw, Butterfly would be disappointed not to meet Winifred and the wallabies before they went onstage, but on the other paw, Ermine really wanted to go. She decided she would – it would only take two minutes and she could ask Winifred for an autograph to give to Butterfly as a surprise.

"Ready?" Butterfly appeared in the doorway with Sylvia.

Ermine stuffed the letter in her pocket guiltily. She grabbed her straw hat, threw her camera over one shoulder and picked up her tool kit. "Ready!" she said.

A little while later, Sylvia, Butterfly and Ermine got off the ferry at the quay.

Ermine looked around anxiously for Eric.

NYOW-WOW-WA-NYOW-WOW-WA-NYOW-WOW-WA!

The sound of the didgeridoo reverberated along her whiskers.

"There he is!" Ermine scurried over to where Eric was entertaining a large crowd. She pushed her way to the front of the group with

Butterfly. They both found their feet tapping in time to the rhythm.

"**Ermine!**" Eric cried when he finished the song. "It's good to see you again! And you must be Butterfly…"

"How do you know that?" asked Butterfly.

Eric smiled. "I've been reading about you in the news. You two are pretty popular round here at the moment. Now what can I do for you?"

"We want you to play for us at *Australia's Most Awesome Animal Show*." Ermine explained her idea to Eric.

"**Pleeeeeeaaaaaaase!**" said Butterfly, when Ermine had finished.

"No worries," Eric said. "I'd be glad to." He picked up the didgeridoo and followed Butterfly and Ermine to where Sylvia was waiting.

Ermine made the introductions. "Sylvia, meet Eric. Eric, meet Sylvia. Sylvia's the world's greatest opera singer," she added by way of explanation. "And Eric's the world's greatest didgeridoo player."

The two grown-ups greeted each other warmly.

"I'm so glad you agreed to play for them," said Sylvia to Eric. "Your music will sound wonderful in the concert hall."

They made their way along the promenade to the Opera House and up the steps. There was a big queue of people waiting to collect their tickets. They waved to Ermine and Butterfly. Ermine and Butterfly waved back. Butterfly even signed a few autographs.

The steward showed them into the concert hall.

Ermine gasped when she saw inside. The hall was like a great cathedral, with rows and rows and rows of seats all around, a huge organ at the back and a fan-shaped roof flooded with light. In front of them was an enormous stage with an orchestra pit below.

"It's amazing," she whispered. "You know, Butterfly, you really *should* go to the opera one day and hear your grandma sing."

"Oh, all right," Butterfly said. "But I'm not going to wear a feathered hat."

The concert hall was filling up quickly. "This way." The steward showed them to the front, where seats had been reserved for them behind the judges. Most of the other competitors were already there.

Paul Piggott and Pete the percussion-playing platypus

Lucy Sponge and Sue the sighing sloth

Bill Trogg and Bert the bearded tarantula

The only ones missing were Winifred
Winnit and her performing wallabies.

WINIFRED WINNIT

WALLABY 1

WALLABY 2

WALLABY 3

They must be waiting for me, thought Ermine. "Back in a minute," she said to Butterfly, wriggling off her seat.

"Where are you going?" Butterfly asked suspiciously.

"To the lavatory," Ermine lied. "I need to…er…wash my whiskers." She scurried off before Butterfly and Sylvia had a chance to stop her.

Sylvia and Butterfly exchanged glances.

"Why do I get the feeling she's up to something?" Sylvia said.

"I'm not sure, but so do I," Butterfly replied. She got down off her seat. "Don't worry, Grandma, you wait there. I'll make sure she's okay."

Chapter 9

At the stage door of the Sydney Opera House...

Winifred Winnit was waiting for Ermine at the stage door. She was wearing her colourful clown outfit with a pair of enormous red shoes and long, candy-striped laces.

"Sorry I'm late!" Ermine panted.

"Never mind!" tinkled Winifred.

"Come and say hello to the team." She led the way to her dressing room, ushered Ermine inside and closed the door firmly behind her.

Ermine was surprised to see the wallabies were penned up in a cage. She was also surprised to see a creature the size of a small dog wearing a gold collar keeping watch on them.

It had a plaster on its nose.

"This is Cruella," Winifred said.

Ermine stared hard at Cruella. There was something familiar about the animal's great jaws and long toes. Come to think of it, there was something familiar about Winifred too.

She peered at her closely.

Underneath Winifred's make-up were traces of black ink.

Then she realized.

Winifred and Cruella were the surfer dude and his dog!

"You were at the aquarium!" she gasped.

Winifred nodded. Her expression had changed. She was looking at Ermine as if she'd just eaten a super-sour sweet.

Ermine felt a little worried. Something told her that Winifred wasn't very pleased to see her after all.

There was an awkward pause.

"I'm sorry about squirting squid ink in your eyes," Ermine said eventually.

"*Are* you?" said Winifred heavily. "What about **squelching** me with a sea cucumber?"

"And that," said Ermine. "Although you must admit it was a silly place to stand."

Winifred glowered at her. "What about using my backside as a pincushion for sea urchins?"

"Now that wasn't my fault…" Ermine began.

AND PRACTICALLY DROWNING ME AT THE SURF COMPETITION?

Winifred's voice rose to a scream. It echoed around the dressing room.

"*Did* I?" Ermine said in a puzzled voice. "I'm afraid I didn't notice. I was having so much fun."

Just then the door flew open. It was Butterfly. She'd been listening through the keyhole.

"What are *you* doing here?" demanded Winifred.

"Never mind that," said Butterfly hotly. "The question is what were *you* doing following *us*? And why were you in disguise?"

"We were trying to catch your little ferrety friend, of course!" Winifred said.

Ermine's whiskers twitched with annoyance. She didn't take kindly to being compared with a ferret. "You mean *me*, I suppose?" she said haughtily. Suddenly she remembered the Duke. "You don't want to make me into a fur collar, do you? Only it's a bit hot for that in Australia, I should say."

Winifred shook her head. "No. I just want you out of the way so that I can be crowned winner of *Australia's Most Awesome Animal Show* one last time, like I deserve." She gave an evil laugh. "Then I can buy a Jacuzzi and finally get rid of these loathsome wallabies."

"You mean you don't like wallabies?" Butterfly said, horrified.

"I HATE wallabies," said Winifred. "And koalas. If one ever kissed me, I'd be SiCk. That goes for stoats too, although you *would* make an excellent duster." She made a grab for Ermine. "Easy peasy, Ermine squeezy!" she cried.

Ermine dodged out of the way.

"COME HERE!" Winifred screamed.
"I WANT YOU TO CLEAN MY HOUSE!"

She made another lunge for Ermine, tripped over her enormous shoes and fell hard on her bottom.

"QUICK, ERMINE, RUN!" shouted Butterfly, holding open the door.

"In a minute!" said Ermine. "First I'm letting the wallabies out."

She scampered past Winifred,

somersaulted off
Cruella's back

and climbed
up the bars
of the cage.

She felt in
her tool kit
and pulled
out a pair of
wire cutters.

"WATCH OUT FOR CRUELLA, ERMINE!"

Butterfly cried.

Ermine glanced round. The Tasmanian devil was just behind her. Clinging on to the wire she grasped the cutters in one paw.

SNIP!

The padlocks fell to the floor and the cage door swung open on Cruella, sending her hurtling into Winifred's lap.

The wallabies bounced out.

Winifred let out a shriek of rage.

"Follow me, wallabies!" Ermine led the way out of the dressing room and along the corridor. Butterfly raced after her with the wallabies. They rushed into the concert hall and onto the stage.

"HURRY, CRUELLA!" Winifred lumbered after them in her enormous shoes, the Tasmanian devil close behind.

Bill Trogg and his bearded
tarantula were just finishing their act.
"MIND BERT!" shouted Bill, as Winifred
mounted the steps.

But it was too late. Winifred's long laces
had become tangled up with the
tarantula's beard. She tripped
over again. This time she
landed face down in the
middle of the stage in
front of the audience.

The tarantula untangled its
beard from her laces and crawled
up her clown suit into her hair.
The audience gasped.

"GET THE STOAT,
CRUELLA!"
Winifred cried.

The audience froze in shock. They couldn't believe what they were seeing. Cameras zoomed in from every angle. All across Australia, the nation was glued to their TV screens.

Cruella advanced on Ermine.

Ermine zigzagged this way and that, but the stage was so crowded with people and wallabies, not to mention Winifred and her enormous shoes she couldn't escape.

"GGGGRRRRRRRRR!"

Cruella opened her great jaws.

"WALLABIES! HELP ERMINE!"

Butterfly cried.

BOING! BOING! BOING!

The wallabies surrounded Cruella, making a tight fence around her with their broad tails.

Cruella growled and
growled, but the wallabies
didn't budge. Now Ermine
and Butterfly had come to their
rescue, they were no longer afraid
of Cruella.

One of the wallabies
gave her a big KICK.
Cruella flew
through the air...

and landed
safely in one of the
drums in the orchestra pit.

"I'LL GET YOU FOR THIS!" Winifred shrieked. She struggled to her feet, the tarantula still on her head, and parted its beard from her eyes. She staggered towards Ermine. "Get out of my way, wallabies," she hissed. "I want that STOAT. This is my competition. MINE!"

Ermine ran up the tail of the biggest wallaby and somersaulted onto its head. "DON'T LISTEN TO HER, WALLABIES!" she shouted.

"This is your competition, not Winifred Winnit's. You're the ones the audience wants to see!"

The audience clapped and cheered. Ermine was right. No one cared about Winifred any more.

To Winifred's astonishment the wallabies pushed past her to the front of the stage and began to **dance**.

Only it wasn't the dance Winifred had taught them. It was the sort of dance they would do together in the wild.

They **tumbled** and **bounced**.

They **twisted** and **sprang**.

They even started **play-boxing**.

They were enjoying themselves so much
that one of them accidentally **biffed** Winifred
on the nose!

Winifred tripped over for a third time.
She fell off the stage and landed in the drum
with Cruella.

"**AAAARRRRRRGGHHHHH!**"

she screamed.

Everyone in the audience
started to laugh.

Butterfly giggled
helplessly.

Ermine leaped from the wallaby's head onto Butterfly's shoulder, pulled out her camera and pointed it towards Winifred. "You don't mind if I get a photo for my scrapbook, do you?" she said with a winning smile. "Only the Duchess said I have to fill it up."

"And now, ladies and gentlemen, the act you have all been waiting for," said the presenter. "From Balaclavia, dancing to the didgeridoo, here's Ermine with her special friends, Eric and Butterfly!"

Eric came up onstage beside Ermine and Butterfly. The wallabies took a bow. Eric placed his didgeridoo in front of him and began to play.

NYOW-WOW-WA-NYOW-WOW-WA-NYOW-WOW-WA

The sound of nature echoed around the concert hall.

Ermine flipped and cartwheeled. She somersaulted and jived. She even did the worm. Butterfly joined in. So did the wallabies and all the other animals in the show. Together they danced and danced to Eric's wonderful music, to the delight of the cheering crowd.

Dear Duchess,

I am having a fantastic time in Sydney. I have made great friends with Sylvia and Butterfly (especially since I rescued Butterfly from Sydney Harbour Bridge). Butterfly is very independent-minded (like me). She has finally agreed to go to the opera tonight to hear Sylvia sing with Luciano Singalotti, although (unlike me) she refuses to wear a feathered hat.

You might have seen on the news that Butterfly and I won Australia's Most Awesome Animal Show thanks to an amazing musician called Eric, who is the world's greatest didgeridoo player. It turns out that last year's winner – Winifred Winnit – didn't even like animals! She tried to stop me from taking part, but my new friends the wallabies came to the rescue just in time and booted Winifred and her horrible pet Tasmanian devil into a drum in the orchestra pit.

Sylvia suggested that I should give the prize money from the show to the Opera House to spend on more projects with Eric and his friends, which I think is a very good idea – but don't worry, I have set aside enough to buy you a present. I thought you might like one of Eric's CDs!

I have also taken lots of photographs and am keeping up-to-date with my scrapbook.

Lots of love, Ermine

PS. Please could you write and tell me where I'm going next on my travels? I think I fancy somewhere with a lot of history...

AUSTRALIA

POSTAGE PAID

SYDNEY
★ ★ ★
POSTAGE

AUSTRALIA

Grand Duchess Maria Von Schnitzel

The Imperial House of Hasbeen

Hasbeen Castle

Balaclavia

Europe

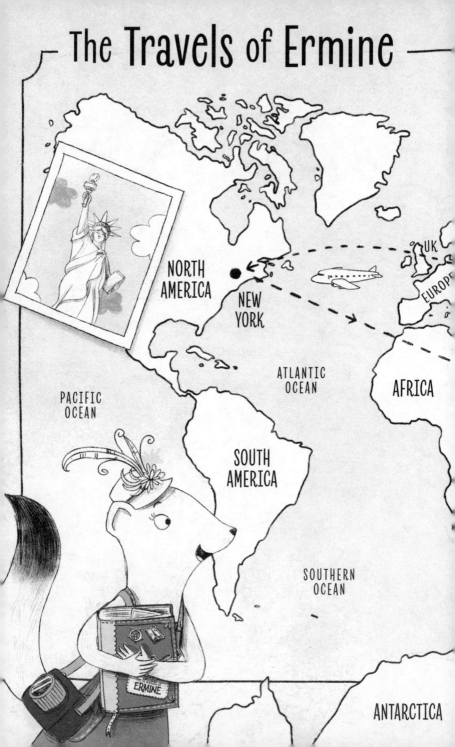

The Travels of Ermine

NORTH AMERICA

NEW YORK

UK

EUROPE

AFRICA

ATLANTIC OCEAN

PACIFIC OCEAN

SOUTH AMERICA

SOUTHERN OCEAN

ANTARCTICA

THE TRAVELS OF ERMINE

ARCTIC OCEAN

N
W — E
S

BALACLAVIA

ASIA

Passenger: Miss E. Stoat
Class: A
From: New York, USA
Destination: Sydney, Australia

Miss E. Stoat
Class: A
From: NYC
To: SYD

PACIFIC OCEAN

INDIAN OCEAN

AUSTRALIA

SYDNEY

Join Ermine on her next adventure!

How to make a travel

Ermine loves sticking photos, tickets, maps, postcards and more in her scrapbook as a way of remembering all the fabulous places she's visited. Why not give it a go yourself?

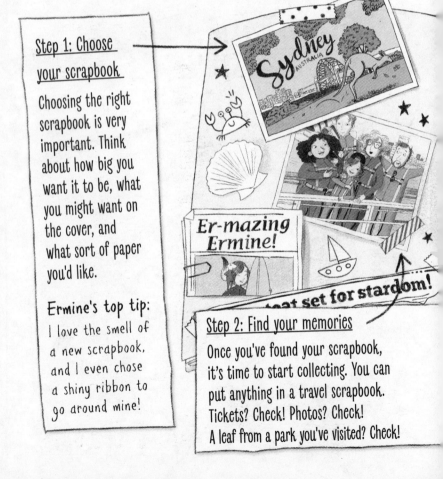

Step 1: Choose your scrapbook

Choosing the right scrapbook is very important. Think about how big you want it to be, what you might want on the cover, and what sort of paper you'd like.

Ermine's top tip: I love the smell of a new scrapbook, and I even chose a shiny ribbon to go around mine!

Sydney
AUSTRALIA

Er-mazing Ermine!

...at set for stardom!

Step 2: Find your memories

Once you've found your scrapbook, it's time to start collecting. You can put anything in a travel scrapbook. Tickets? Check! Photos? Check! A leaf from a park you've visited? Check!

scrapbook like Ermine

Step 3: Stick it down

Now you're happy with the layout of your page, it's time to start sticking things down!

Ermine's top tip:
If I've used glue, I always leave my pages to dry out before closing my scrapbook.

Australia

Surfing stoat takes Sydney by storm!

SYDNEY

Step 4: Travel!

Decide where you want to travel to next...

Ermine's top tip:
I love to explore – from new countries and cities, to my own home, the outdoors, indoors and anywhere else I fancy. All you need is a dash of determination, a sprinkle of courage, and a dollop of curiosity!

Ermine's top tip:
I always place everything on the page first, so I can move things around and make sure I'm happy with how it looks!

Happy travels!

To everyone
who made my trip to
Australia truly Ermazing.
Jennifer

To my beloved niece, Shiama,
who has just been on a great
adventure in Sydney like our
heroine Ermine. *Elisa*

First published in the UK in 2018 by Usborne Publishing Ltd., Usborne House,
83-85 Saffron Hill, London EC1N 8RT, England. www.usborne.com

Text copyright © Jennifer Gray, 2018
The right of Jennifer Gray to be identified as the author of this work has been
asserted by her in accordance with the Copyright, Designs and Patents Act, 1988.

Illustrations copyright © Usborne Publishing Ltd., 2018
Illustrations by Elisa Paganelli.

The name Usborne and the devices ♛ ♛ are Trade Marks of Usborne Publishing Ltd.

A CIP catalogue record for this book is available from the British Library.

JFMAM JASOND/18

ISBN 9781474927260   04334/1
Printed in the UK.